NOBODY LEFT BEHIND

ONE CHILD'S STORY ABOUT TESTING

Deanna Enos

*Best Wishes
Deanna Enos
8-13-08*

iUniverse, Inc.
New York Lincoln Shanghai

NOBODY LEFT BEHIND
ONE CHILD'S STORY ABOUT TESTING

iUniverse books may be ordered through booksellers or by contacting:

iUniverse
2021 Pine Lake Road, Suite 100
Lincoln, NE 68512
www.iuniverse.com
1-800-Authors (1-800-288-4677)

ISBN-13: 978-0-595-38293-4 (pbk)
ISBN-13: 978-0-595-82664-3 (ebk)
ISBN-10: 0-595-38293-2 (pbk)
ISBN-10: 0-595-82664-4 (ebk)

Printed in the United States of America

To my grandchildren, so that they can always know their grandma wrote a book.

ACKNOWLEDGMENTS

I wish to thank all the children who helped me to understand the struggles they were having with test anxiety. They have given me the desire to make their voices heard.

My gratitude to my writing friends in Fortuna, who kept me inspired by their own good writing and perseverance.

My special appreciation to Bunny Bassett, Jean Murray, and Claudia Nelson, who knew of this project and helped me not to let go of it.

PREFACE

Storytelling is one way to begin dialogue among children, teachers, and parents about a subject that is very important to all of them. That is how *Nobody Left Behind* came to be. Test anxiety is a tremendous problem for some children. Testing has a lasting effect on schools, how they get their funding, and how they provide learning since accountability has become a top priority. It also has a lasting effect on children, and they need to understand more about it.

Ignored fears grow. Test results are final answers. Children benefit from fewer final answers about them and from more people believing in their potential.

ELEMENTS OF THE BOOK

The beginning of each chapter includes a quote by a famous person. Each quote specifically applies to the chapter that follows it.

There are eighteen chapters, each one developing the nine-year-old's point of view as he struggles with his situation.

There are questions at the end pertaining to each chapter and activities for art and writing to expand the child's creative ability and help him or her understand the predicament. Special test-taking tips are also included.

CONTENTS

When we are young
we want a great deal more of life
than we do of school.
Robert Frost

CHAPTER 1

"Time to get up, Jeff."

Nine-year-old Jeffery Taylor pulled the pillow over his head in an attempt to block out the dreaded sound that meant he had to get up. Monday morning was school, and he hated school.

The same old thing. He wanted to do something different today. School was boring. He wished his dad had taken him on the fishing boat, but his mother wouldn't allow it.

"I have my reasons," she'd said when he asked once why he couldn't go. "You'd rather be out playing, for sure, but life isn't all fun and games, you know. There's work involved—and school."

As he sat up, Jeff reached for his clock. He'd set his alarm the previous night, but this morning it had failed to ring, so now he had to listen to his mother's sharp voice. "Jeff, get out of that bed!"

More important to him than getting up was the fact that the clock hadn't rung. He picked it up and examined it. It was ticking. The button was pulled out.

"I wonder…I wonder why," he thought. He gazed at the clock, taking time to watch the second hand go around several times.

He pulled back the lever of the clock to see if the alarm would go off. Then he made the clock swoop as if it were a plane in flight and hummed to himself. His feet still had not hit the floor. He was avoiding the inevitable. What he really wanted was to have it be Saturday. No such luck.

Jeff's mother's third call got results. Jeff gently set the clock on the nightstand and, throwing back the covers, climbed out of bed. It didn't matter to him what he wore, so he grabbed the faded blue jeans and crumpled yellow T-shirt that were lying limply on a chair under the window.

Jeff was an only child, so the loft bedroom in the remodeled house was his own. His mother sometimes went up there, mostly just to change the sheets on his single bed, which was shoved against the wall under the sloped ceiling. He had more than his share of toys stuffed in his closet, toys that he no longer played with much.

His bookshelves were lined with miniature soldiers that had once belonged to his dad. Jeff spent hours arranging and rear-ranging the little figures. They were closer to him than his dad had ever been.

Jeff felt safe in his room. Nothing changed there unless he changed it. His soldiers always stayed exactly where he left them.

"Are you up yet?" It was his mother again. He heard but did-n't answer.

"What's so important about dumb old school? Boring stuff. The same thing over and over: reading, math, spelling; reading, math, spelling. Who cares about all that junk? They give us all these papers to color. They never even let us draw. Hardly ever." He reached for his clock.

"I wish this clock could change the day. I wish this clock could change the day," he chanted, marching down the stairs.

His mother's voice hit him like the gunshots of a firing squad he'd seen on TV.

"Jeff, why didn't you change your clothes?" Shaking her head and sighing heavily, she banged a glass on the table, spilling the juice. "You march right back upstairs and change immediately," she ordered.

Without hesitation, Jeff turned around and stomped up the stairs to do as he was told.

"I wish today was Saturday. I wish, I wish, I wish," he muttered to himself.

As he entered the room, Jeff eyed his clock and grinned. "I'll bet there's an army living in there," he thought to himself. "Aha! Last night, while I was sleeping, they moved in and dismantled every little screw and lever. Maybe they're marching around, plotting a secret way to change time."

"That's it! That's it! That must be it!" he repeated aloud.

"Jeffrey Taylor, get down here, now!"

He was hopping on one foot, trying to get the other foot out of his pants, and managed to get all tangled up in the long laces. Finally, he yanked off the shoes and found some brown corduroy pants and a clean blue sweatshirt.

Dressed once again, he stepped back into his high-tops, tugging at them with one hand and reaching for the clock with the other. He grabbed a brush and took a swipe at his light brown hair. He then tossed the brush toward the bed, clomped down the stairs, and headed for the hall closet, where he placed the cherished timepiece into a jacket pocket. He slipped his arms into the coat sleeves.

Still standing, he crunched his Cheerios while leaning over the kitchen table. When he finished, he trudged out to the car where his mother, searching for keys in her overstuffed purse, didn't notice his new expression of excitement. He kept his hand firmly on the clock in his jacket pocket. It was his secret weapon, a trigger for his imagination.

"It's almost nine," his mother said. "We'll be late again."

'Tis the mind
that makes the body rich.
William Shakespeare

CHAPTER 2

Jeff opened the car door and started to get into the seat next to his mother.

"Not that seat, Jeff," his mother said. "We're not going to take any chances with the air bag."

Jeff hated sitting in the backseat. It was hard to see over the tall front seat's headrest. He'd never seen an air bag, so its existence wasn't real to him.

"I hate sitting in the back," he griped. "Why can't I stay here?"

"No, Jeff. Hop in the back. We haven't got time to argue about it now. Just do as I say."

"Oh, all right." Jeff slammed the front door and reached for the back door handle. The door wouldn't open.

"I can't get in," he said, as his mother stuck the key in the ignition and started the motor. She quickly released the safety latch, allowing Jeff to jump into the car shortly before she started backing out of the driveway.

Jeff leaned back against the seat and looked at the back of his mother's head. He sat without speaking.

"Put on your seatbelt, Jeff," his mother said in an automatic voice that Jeff heard very often these days. He did not know why his mother had to be so bossy.

"What is it with grown-ups? They don't ever have time for anything important. I'd rather see her face and talk to her than have to look at the back of her head," he thought.

Jeff pulled the clock from his pocket. He felt really proud to have his own timepiece. He placed it to his ear and listened to the rhythm of the ticking. The gentle sound blocked out the whole confusing world. He didn't hear the traffic noises or the frustrated comments from his mother as she tried to explain about the child killed by the impact of the air bag while sitting in the front seat.

As he stared at the clock, Jeff saw the front glass begin to open. It was a shiny door and not a glass at all. He could still hear the ticking and it became louder to him. The second hand moved with a jerky motion, and Jeff imagined himself sitting on it, going for a ride.

The hum of the car motor soothed him as he allowed his imagination to enjoy the motion. He pretended that he was holding on to the end while swinging out to catch the minute hand. Now *that* would not be easy. Oops, he missed. Now he'd have to wait until it went around again.

He heard other noises coming from inside the clock. He thought about why it had not rung. If his friends inside the clock could change time, maybe other things could change too. Maybe all clocks could change. Maybe inventors of clocks could change. Maybe grown-ups could stop thinking of time as something more important than other things.

The car stopped abruptly, startling Jeff into reality. The school.

"Bye, Jeff," said his mother. "Go directly home after class. Do you have your key?"

"It's here," Jeff grabbed for the chain around his neck.

"See you around five thirty." Ruth Taylor eased the car forward, leaving Jeff to face his dreaded fate: school.

Education isn't play and it can't
be made to look like play.
It is hard, hard work.
It can be made interesting work.
Thomas Edison

CHAPTER 3

Carol Radner, the fourth grade teacher at George McGowan Elementary School, was getting ready for the day to begin. She was organizing the pile of achievement tests spread out on her desk.

"The curse of the educational system," she mumbled. Principal Morrison had left them in her room that morning.

"Here are some of your tests," he'd said. "I'll bring the others in later, and we'll start giving them on Wednesday."

By nine o'clock the room was filled with children, but one seat remained empty. Jeffrey Taylor was late again.

"Good morning, children. Shall we stand for the pledge?"

Miss Radner placed her hand over her heart and began to clearly enunciate the words, "I pledge allegiance to the flag..." Part of the way through, a car stopped outside. Miss Radner paused, gave a brief sigh, and completed the salute. She glanced at the stack of tests lying on her desk.

"The morning math drill is on the board," she said. "Copy the problems correctly. You have two minutes to complete them, so work carefully and efficiently. Do your best."

The children did exactly as they were told, except for Matt Huggins. He stuck his tongue out at Miss Radner and scribbled something on his paper before he slipped it in his desk. Miss Radner didn't look up from where she was working. Some of the children were counting fingers; others were trying to count in their heads, moving their eyes back and forth as they did so; and a few wrote answers from memory. The tension in the room was as strained as twenty-five rubber bands ready to snap. Miss Radner moved toward the teacher's aide who was correcting papers at a table near the door.

"We'll be giving the tests this Wednesday," she whispered.

"Oh, already?" Mary Jo whispered back. "Pressure, pressure, pressure."

"Sad, isn't it? Poor kids! They don't get to be kids for long these days." Both women shook their heads with a gesture of resignation. "It's not like we have anything to say about it."

"This ain't great. This I hate. Radner gets me when I'm late." Jeff chanted as he bounded up the front steps, touching every other one. The clock bulging in his coat pocket gave him comfort. He was glad he had it with him. It was doing more than just telling time. Its rhythm was his comfort.

The front door was heavy, and Jeff tugged it open to face a narrow, empty hallway. Bulletin boards tacked here and there and covered with faded construction paper reminded Jeff that excellent papers always had a place to go. He didn't want his papers stuck out here in this ugly, deserted spot. He stepped toward his classroom and then stopped. With his right hand, he pulled the clock from his pocket and slipped it into his left hand. He wound it several times, placed it to his ear, and listened to the gentle ticking sound. He closed his eyes, enjoying the steady beat of the reliable rhythm.

When he opened his eyes, he was again confronted with that tunnel leading directly to a place he did not want to go. Reluctantly, he headed for the great, gray door marked "4," and he pulled it open.

A million blobs were bowed at work, and a big, tall monster with a squawking, screeching voice yelled, "Jeff, you're late!" The words dissected his brain.

Jeff only heard, "You're late!" His face turned red, and his eyes flashed as his thoughts escaped to the special little people he imagined in his clock. "Shall I tell her why I was late today?"

Excitedly, he blurted out, "Miss Radner, can I share something about my clock?"

"Not now, Jeff. Do the morning math drill first. You can tell us about your clock later. First things first."

He heard, "Not now."

He laid his head down on the desk, oblivious that the other children were finishing and handing in their papers to the smiling Miss Radner. He lifted his head and stared out the window.

"Jeffrey, get busy," Miss Radner whispered in her prodding, frustrated voice. "No daydreaming!"

He heard, "Get busy." He opened his desk immediately, glad to be hidden from critical eyes. From his blue folder, he took out a piece of clean, white paper. Spying his felt pens, he grabbed them too, as the spark of an idea took hold of him. No longer aware of where he was, Jeff closed his desk and started to draw. With a thin-line black felt marking pen, he sketched the outline of several tiny characters. He drew rapidly—in his mind's eye he saw the figures on the paper even before he put them there. He reached for the colored pens and added the color he was imagining.

Nobody interrupted him. Jeff could hear a voice in the background saying something about papers and spelling, but it sounded far away. The drawing was real and alive. The figures marched to the rhythm of his clock.

The voice grew louder, finally forcing Jeff back to Miss Radner's classroom. "Jeff, I need to see you out in the hall for a moment."

Jeff lifted his drawing and, clutching it against him, followed his teacher out the door. He rushed past Matt Huggins's desk, trying to avoid hearing his jeering remarks.

"Jeff's in trouble. Jeff's in trouble."

He knew he was in for it when he looked at Miss Radner's face. "Jeff, you were late again this morning. You haven't done any of your math, and now I catch you sitting there drawing. You don't pay any attention to what I say to you. I'm trying to help you, but you make it impossible."

"I know," Jeff mumbled. "But I like to draw. I'm good at it."

"I know, Jeff, but the math is more important."

"See what I drew," Jeff thrust his picture forward. It was a mass of color, motion, and design. Vivid reds, bright blues, yellows, and oranges—all detailed in black outlines. Miss Radner's eyes skimmed the surface of the paper, but she didn't *see* any of it.

"Following directions is more important, Jeff. Your drawing is nice, but it isn't what I asked you to do."

Jeff heard, "It's nice." He looked at Miss Radner.

"I knew you'd like it," he said. "It's a picture of my clock, and it shows what went on inside it while I was sleeping. I haven't finished yet, but I drew the people in there busy organizing the levers to change the time." Jeff's imagination had taken over.

"Oh, Jeff," Miss Radner sighed, "I hate to tell you this, but that imagination of yours is going to get you nothing but trouble. Believe me, there's more to life than playing. There are tests, Jeff. Achievement tests. Drawing will never prepare you for taking tests. I'm trying to prepare you for that."

"Can I go finish this now, Miss Radner? It won't take me long, and then I'll do my math. I promise."

"You haven't heard a word I've said. No, Jeff, no. You may not finish that now." She seized the drawing. "I care enough about you to not let you get away with this undisciplined behavior. You will do your math assignment now. No recess until you finish. Do you understand?"

He understood clearly, but he didn't want her to have his drawing. He hesitantly reached for it, and Miss Radner reluctantly released the paper, demanding that he "put it away!"

Jeff cradled his drawing and took it back to his desk, where he carefully placed it under his blue folder.

Great works are performed
not by strength
but by perseverance.
Samuel Johnson

CHAPTER 4

Miss Radner wasn't bad, Jeff decided. After all, she could have ripped up the drawing, but she didn't. She didn't send him to the principal's office. She didn't even make him stand out in the hall all by himself.

He watched the class file out to recess but couldn't join them; he had math to do. He looked at the board. Rows and rows of numbers. He didn't want to look at them. They made his stomach queasy. He could hardly decipher one from the other.

"I'd better copy them in order. Stay in order," he thought. "I wonder why Miss Radner thinks this is so much more important than what I was doing."

The numbers meant nothing to Jeff. He wanted to please Miss Radner, but he couldn't see any value in solving all those problems. It was boring to write numbers, and he didn't want to do it.

He began to write. As he copied the first few numbers, he felt fine. It wasn't bad; he knew how to add. Then he looked back at the board and noticed that the number there did not look exactly like his. The nine was more like a curve. He tried to write it more perfectly. He rewrote the nine, and it looked better, but he noticed the smudge his erasing had left on his paper. Miss Radner would gripe about it being messy. She was mad at him anyway. He could tell by her bossy eyes.

Jeff grabbed the paper, crumpled it, and threw it into the wastebasket. He took out a clean sheet of paper. Looking at the blank page, he visualized his clock people again in their brightly colored regalia. The image didn't last long. He was startled back to math by looking up and seeing Miss Radner's firm expression.

Sighing, he put his name on the paper and wrote the word *math* at the top. He realized that recess was almost over and that he had done nothing. He hastily wrote three problems and dropped his pencil. The noise got Miss Radner's attention.

"Be careful, Jeff!" she said.

Slowly, Jeff picked up the pencil. "Slavery," he thought. "Who was her slave last year? It's too much work for nothing." His heart thumped. His face reddened. He felt trapped. "Escape to the bathroom. That's it. Miss Radner always allows bathroom privileges."

"May I go to the bathroom?" he asked.

"All right, Jeff, but come directly back to the classroom when you're finished."

"Okay," he said grudgingly.

When Jeff entered the hall at recess, he didn't join the others. Matt Huggins was taking charge of the ball game, and Jeff didn't want to play. With eyes looking at the ground, he walked away.

He noticed a spider crawling along the edge of the sidewalk. He bent and then squatted down to get a closer look. He was entranced by the way the spider moved. It had an incredible design on its back and eight long legs. "How does it know which leg to move?" he thought. "When you have that many legs, it must be complicated to decide. If it moved all the legs on one side, would it move at all or would the other side hold it back? Maybe it would just go round in a circle."

The bell rang before Jeff even got to the bathroom. He didn't really need to go there anyway, so he decided to return to the classroom before the others. At least then Miss Radner wouldn't complain.

He knew none of the other kids had seen his spider at recess. Not Matt Huggins. He would have squashed it for sure. Matt was a jerk. He tried to convince everybody that he knew everything, so he didn't really ever have to try. Any time he missed a word in spelling and was corrected, he'd say, "I knew that. I just wanted to see if you knew it." He was a pain in the neck, full of dirty tricks. How he got away with it was beyond Jeff.

The day dragged on, but Jeff finished his math and was the first one out the door when the bell rang at three o'clock.

Kindness is the golden chain
by which society
is bound together.
Goethe

CHAPTER 5

Outside the schoolyard gate, Jeff breathed a sigh of relief. To him, the day was just beginning. For a little while, his time was his own. Since his mother had started her new job, he had had to walk home after school. He didn't mind that though, for it gave him time to go down by the old Wilson house, past the apple orchard, and over the bridge. The creek below was full of water this time of year, and there were fish swimming about. Though he'd never caught any, he knew that someday he would.

His mother didn't get home until five thirty, so he had plenty of time to do what he wanted, and that meant exploring. He loved to explore.

The last time he'd gone near the old house, he'd found something in the yard. At first, he wasn't sure what it was. Cautiously, he'd turned it over and over in his hands, watching the sunlight reflect off of its sharp, chipped surfaces. It had to have been a real arrowhead, like those he'd seen pictures of at the library. He had climbed up the steps, sat down, and leaned against the porch railing. He had closed his fist tightly and wondered whether some great warrior had perhaps dropped this object while hunting. The dark weapon had lain on the ground for years and years until he had discovered it.

Before he knew it, the sun had gone down and he had to run all the way home.

This day, he decided to sit on the bridge and dangle his legs over the edge. It was a long way down to the water. He spit to see whether his saliva would make a ripple when it hit the water. It did. Then he tossed in a rock. That made a bigger wave on the water's surface. He noticed a leaf floating and reached for a stick. Aiming at the leaf, he threw the stick and watched as it hit the leaf and moved downstream. He thought about getting his feet wet, but decided against it. That would have meant climbing down the hill, and he wasn't that ambitious. He was content remaining where he was. Leaves were falling about him, and he wondered what it would be like to be a leaf floating from a tree down into the water. It sure looked like it might be fun.

Jeff leaned farther over the rail until he could see his reflection in the moving water. He looked distorted and weird. Putting his hands up and wiggling his fingers, he observed the strangeness of the images below. He was so engrossed that he didn't hear the old man walk up beside him.

The elderly fellow stood observing him for several minutes before he leaned over to cast his reflection in the water next to Jeff.

"See any fish?" he asked.

"No," answered Jeff, startled by the voice that broke into his quiet. "I guess I'd better go," he thought, remembering that his mom had told him not to talk to strangers.

"Do you come here often?" the old man inquired.

"Should I tell him?" he wondered. Jeff stared at the chubby, peculiar individual standing before him. "Could be some-body's grandpa," he thought. "He's not mean looking with those twinkling eyes. I wonder where he got that shabby, plaid coat and that scrunched-up seedy, green hat." Jeff felt awkward. He'd seen lots of homeless old people on TV lately. That's what the old man looked like. Jeff stood up next to the aged vagabond. He smelled like he could use a bath, but he appeared to need somebody to talk to.

"What's your name, fella?" the old man asked.

Jeff thought of the story he'd heard about Captain Smudge and how in the end it said, *Remember if you ever see anyone different from you, be kind.*

"My name is Jeff," he responded, determined to appear calm. "He is a stranger," Jeff thought, "and Mom said I should-n't talk to strangers, but he looks so lonely."

The old man pulled off his hat and began to rub his bald head. "I used to fish in a creek like this years ago, when I was about your size. That was a mighty long time ago. Let's see, I must have been about ten years old then. Me and my brother, sometimes we'd skip school and sneak down to that creek, and boy we'd catch the biggest fish." His eyes glistened as he spoke.

Nobody had ever talked to Jeff about sneaking out of school before. He'd never even considered that. But this old man had a story to tell, and Jeff wanted to hear it. "I guess school was no better when he was a boy," Jeff thought. "I wonder what it was really like then?"

There was no need to ask, because the old fellow kept right on talking. He didn't care whether Jeff was hearing him or not. He was remembering days long gone, a picture clear in his mind.

Jeff concentrated on what was being said, but got so concerned about how he was saying it that he couldn't hear a word. He noticed that the man never stopped using his hands as he talked. The old man's head was constantly shaking as if he was agreeing with his every word.

The more Jeff looked at him, the sadder he became. He started to think about his own grandpa, who had died just the year before. His had been a quick death, and the loss still hurt.

For a moment, he thought that his grandpa had returned, and he wanted to hug the old guy. Then he thought again about what his mother had said about strangers.

It had been a rough day for Jeff at school, and he knew that he should be getting home. He took the clock out of his jacket pocket. The old man kept talking and looking at Jeff with such need that Jeff didn't know what he should do.

"I guess I'd better go now," Jeff said. "It's getting late."

"Which way are you going?"

"Down Jameson Road. See you." With that, Jeff placed the clock to his ear and ran toward his house, about fifteen minutes away. He didn't look back, for if he had, he might have been tempted to stay.

Without art
the crudeness of reality
would make the world
unbearable.
George Bernard Shaw

CHAPTER 6

The house was empty when Jeff returned home. Nothing new. He reached down into his shirt and pulled out his key. It briefly got stuck in the lock, but he finally got the door open. He headed straight for the refrigerator, got a glass of milk, and made some raisin toast. He switched on the TV and plopped down on the sofa. He missed not having his mother there to greet him, but he knew that she had to work now that his dad was gone. He knew that she'd be coming home soon.

About two bites into his second piece of toast, the phone rang. It was his mother.

"I'm sorry, Jeff, but some things have come up here at work, and I'm going to be a little late. Be sure to lock the doors and take some hamburger out of the freezer. I'll get there as soon as I can. Is everything all right?"

"Everything's fine," he said before he slowly hung up the phone.

She had been late lots of times, and Jeff was getting used to it. He missed the good old days when his mom and dad were both home more. Now Dad was away working on a fishing boat, and Mom was down at the dental office. The house was empty. He swallowed the last bite of his toast and reached for a pencil. Doodling was one way to cope.

His drawing began slowly, but his enthusiasm for it increased and eventually he no longer heard the TV. He no longer thought about being home alone or about his rotten day at school. He drew a simple figure of an old man in a plaid overcoat and a scrunched-up hat. The man's arms were up as if he were moving them. Jeff concentrated on drawing the bridge, remembering how it looked. He loved that bridge more than any other place. It was his special spot.

Jeff began to wonder about the old man he'd met. Did he live near the bridge? Did he have a family? Why did he look so sad? Why did he talk so much? Where did he get that coat? The more Jeff thought about him, the clearer the drawing became. He added details, sharpening lines and shadows. Time flew, and before he knew it, his mother came rushing through the door, tossed her purse on a chair, and headed for the kitchen.

"Let's get some dinner going, Jeff. You must be starving. I'm sorry that I'm so late. Last-minute emergency. Patient broke a tooth." She washed her hands.

"Oh, that's all right, Mom. I had some toast."

"What have you been doing since you got home?"

"Drawing."

"Drawing? What were you drawing? Didn't you have any homework? You always have math."

"Not tonight. I finished all my math at school, and for once Miss Radner didn't give me more."

"Oh, that's nice. Where's the mustard? Why don't you put the catsup on the table, too?"

Jeff decided to forget about Miss Radner. A juicy hamburger was more important. He could hear his stomach growling as his mother moved hastily about the kitchen, preparing the food. She quickly turned and plopped the meat on his sliced bun. Jeff poured mustard, mayonnaise, and catsup on top of his burger. He liked the way the colors blended. He shoved the other part of the bun on top, then took it off to see the design.

"Jeff, don't play with your food."

He set the bun back and took a bite. He was content for the moment to sit with his mother in his own house and fill his stomach. He remembered how his dad had teased him about having a hollow leg. Jeff didn't think so, but he did have an empty place inside him without his dad around. They ate most of the meal in silence, as his mother seemed preoccupied with other thoughts. She was probably worrying about some problem at work. Somebody's teeth no doubt. He wanted to tell her about the picture he'd done at school, but she just didn't seem like she'd be interested. She might give him another lecture about schoolwork.

Drawing was important, but nobody understood that. Nobody knew how much it meant to him. Could he show her the illustration of the old man? No. Then she would want to know who he was, and he'd have to say that he had talked to a stranger after school. That would surely upset her. He'd had enough upsets for one day.

By eight thirty, Jeff was ready for bed. When he got to his room, he sat down for a moment and looked at the picture he had drawn. He had really liked the old man, and he took a little more time to finish his drawing. He got out his pajamas and thought about the clock in his jacket pocket. He took it out and set it on the bedside table. "I'm tired," he thought, as he pulled off his clothes and put on his pj's. "Today was pretty cool, meeting the old man by the bridge. I sure hope I see him again."

I seek my inspiration in the real.
It lays hold on my imagination,
stirs it and gives it new life.
Pablo Picasso

CHAPTER 7

As luck would have it, Jeff wasn't late the next day; therefore, Miss Radner wasn't grouchy. At least she wasn't annoyed until about ten o'clock, when Principal Morrison rushed into the room and plopped more booklets onto her desk.

"Test time," he said. "I hope you've been a good teacher, and that they're prepared. We've got to send the tests off to be corrected on Friday, so you'd better start them this afternoon. They get these tests to us so early, you almost wish we still had the pony express."

Miss Radner smiled, but her expression betrayed her true feelings. She felt as though she had been hit by the mail truck. Obviously this was a big disruption in her plans, and she glanced in her plan book to see what she had hoped to accomplish.

She strolled to the window and shoved it open to let in some fresh air. She turned to her class and, in her gentlest voice, asked everyone to put away the papers and books on their desks.

"Did you all hear Principal Morrison? These are the achievement tests, and today we must begin them. You may line up to sharpen your no. 2 pencils."

Jeff rummaged around in his desk to locate his pencil and walked to the line where more than half the others had already arrived.

Tests. Oh, how he hated these tests. They were so long and hard. He remembered when he was in kindergarten, and he had tried to do what his teacher said. But trying so hard always made him the last one to finish. There were so many things he didn't understand then, but he couldn't ask because the teacher had said, "I can't help you." He had thought teachers were there to help you up until that time. He had cried when he got to a section he couldn't do because the teacher had said to go right on to the next question if you didn't know the answer. He'd never done that before. He'd always asked a question when he didn't understand something. Tests just weren't fair.

As he got older, he handled the situation much better, he thought. He didn't read all of the test, but he marked the little circles as if he had. That way he finished first and he'd walk up and hand in the booklet or close it so everybody would see that he was done. It was embarrassing to be slow, so he'd found a way to hide that fact and it seemed worth it.

It caught up with him later when the results came in and his mom got upset. But even that was better than having all the other kids see how slow he was.

With pencils sharpened and everyone seated, Miss Radner passed out the dreaded pages and the ordeal began.

"You may open your test booklet to page 1." She sounded more like a robot than Miss Radner. "Make sure you under-stand all the directions before you begin. Do not begin any test until you are told to do so. Work as fast as you can."

"Easy for her to say," he thought.

"There may be items you cannot do because they have not yet been taught."

"So why give me a test on them if you haven't taught them to me?"

"If an item is too difficult, do not spend too much time on it. Make the most careful choice you can, and go on to the next item."

"You bet I will," he thought.

"You have twenty minutes to complete the first section. Ready…begin."

There was a rustle of papers. Jeff began marking the little dots on the answer sheet. He read very little. Within minutes, he completed the first page and was on to the second. This was a breeze. Dark little pencil dots in a pattern. He didn't care what score he got on this stupid old test. "Poor Miss Radner. She's going to look like a lousy teacher when I get all this stuff wrong. It's dumb anyway, and if she won't help me, why should I help her?"

He finished long before Miss Radner's mechanical voice announced, "Everybody stop."

For five minutes, Jeff had been gazing out the window watching a blue jay flitting about in a nearby tree. It flew back and forth from one branch to another. Jeff thought it was trying to get his attention.

"Birds are so free," he thought. "They don't have to take tests. If only I could be a bird. I would take off any old time— soar high in the sky, land on a wire, and look down on everything." The closest he'd ever come to feeling like a bird was the day he'd climbed the apple tree by the old Wilson house and sat there for the whole afternoon. There had been a cool breeze blowing that made a rustling sound in the leaves. The sun had warmed his face, and he had wanted to stay there forever.

"Ready…begin."

He was supposed to be doing the next test. Hurriedly, he turned the page and began marking dots again. Looking at his answer sheet full of little pencil marks gave him nausea and made him dizzy. He stopped writing. "Miss Radner, may I go to the bathroom?" he asked.

"Shh, Jeff, not now. You're being timed. You'll have to make up the test later if you leave now. Just finish. Then you may go."

"All right," said Jeff. "Boy, you can't even go to the bathroom."

He wrote faster than ever, only pretending to read the questions. By the time he had finished, he knew that he didn't really need to go to the bathroom anyway.

Matt Huggins was still working, and so were most of the other kids. Matt was good at doing tests. He didn't even have to try. Everything came easy for him. He was a brat, though, and the teacher's pet. He was so nice to Miss Radner when she was looking, but behind her back he'd make fun of her and call her names like Big Bad Rad. She thought he was a perfect angel. Jeff knew better.

Jeff started to draw again on a piece of scratch paper next to his test paper. He drew the blue jay that he'd just seen outside the window. He wished it would return.

"Will the first person in each row collect the tests and put them on my desk?"

It was back. Jeff noticed the blue jay perched on the window ledge hopping back and forth. It looked hungry, which made Jeff remember his lunch. He took a tiny bit of his sandwich and tossed it carefully toward the open windowsill. The bird flew away at the motion of his arm but returned to get the treat. It then flew off as quickly as it'd come. Jeff leaned as far as he dared in his seat without falling to try to glimpse the bird in motion. It flew in jerky spurts just the way it did when it hopped on the ground looking for food. Jeff was so absorbed in observing that he didn't even hear the ring of the recess bell.

The children filed outside, carrying bats, balls, ropes, and snacks. Their noisy chattering invaded his quiet reflection.

"Come on, Jeff," yelled Terry, not waiting for his response. Jeff held on to his sandwich sure that during this recess he would locate that blue jay.

The schoolyard was so noisy that the bird avoided the commotion. Jeff watched the sky and then ran to the tree, but he saw nothing. Slowly, he ate his sandwich, keeping a few little crusts in his bag just in case his friend should return to the window.

"Hey, Jeff," shouted Terry, "Why don't you be on our team?"

"No," answered Jeff. "I'm waiting for someone."

"Gee, Jeff. You're no fun anymore," Terry shouted as he ran off to join the others playing on the soccer field.

Jeff and Terry had once been so close that they would often trade shoes. Now Terry was Mr. Hotshot. He was smart and good at sports, and he got to do everything he wanted. He had even joined the swim team and swam every day at after-school practices. Jeff's mom couldn't let Jeff join too because the overnight trips the team traveled on cost too much money.

Back in the classroom, Miss Radner decided to give the class a break. "Since our day has been disrupted, and you had to concentrate so hard this morning on the testing, you may have choice time. You can play games quietly, read, or draw."

"Draw," Jeff repeated aloud and then added to himself, "That Miss Radner is definitely okay."

He eagerly reached for his pencil to resume drawing the picture of the blue jay. He stared at the windowsill for a few moments, visualizing his little friend. He carefully added detail on the head, the rounded body, and the tail feathers. He paid special attention to the feet and even sketched in the bread crumbs. It was a gorgeous creature. He loved that bird, and he wished it would come back to the window again.

Just as he thought that, the blue jay appeared in the window. Jeff couldn't tell for sure whether it was his blue jay, but it was definitely blue. It flew in and circled overhead, confused by the sudden commotion in the room when the children saw it.

"Oh," screamed Miss Radner. "Dear me. We have a guest, I see." She tried to keep calm, but she was obviously unnerved by the presence of this unexpected intruder in her classroom.

The bird circled and swooped, perched and hopped. Jeff was delighted. It was positively the best moment of his day—especially when he looked over at the pile of tests sitting on Miss Radner's desk and noticed that in all the excitement the bird had managed to leave several droppings like spattered bull's-eyes on the top copy.

He laughed about that all the way home. They never did get the blue jay out of the room, so Miss Radner decided that it would be okay to feed it. She even read them a book about birds and their eating habits.

"I might as well turn it into a science lesson," she resolved.

It had turned out to be a pretty good day at school after all…the best one yet this year.

He is the happiest,
be he king or peasant,
who finds peace in his home.
Goethe

CHAPTER 8

That night, Jeff went to his room at eight o'clock. He'd seen *Star Trek* earlier, but now his mother was watching CNN, and he didn't want to watch with her. He'd had enough news about homeless people and killings in far-off places.

He dangled his legs off the side of his bed, listened to the ticking sound his clock made as he wound it, and looked across the room at his soldiers.

He wondered whether his dad was warm and asleep on the fishing boat. He'd been gone for months. Up to Alaska. Where's Alaska? When he'd asked his mom, she hadn't given him a straight answer.

"Oh, it's someplace way up north." She obviously didn't want to talk about it.

He'd remembered the fights that took place when they thought he was asleep.

"Then get out. We can manage without you!" he'd heard his mom yell.

Jeff heard his dad pack his bag and slam the door as he left.

Jeff shook in his bed that night and cried himself to sleep. He wondered whether it was his fault they were fighting.

Since then, his mom had had to work hard to pay for the house. She was always tired. Jeff once tried to tell Terry about it, but Terry didn't understand. His parents were together.

Jeff felt like he didn't have a dad because he never saw him. He did receive a few postcards, and he saved them all in his bedside table.

Dear Jeff,

We had a big catch today. It's very cold here. The boat is working fine and we have a good crew.

Love,

Dad

The cards were always the same and never included a return address where Jeff could write back to him. Jeff felt like his dad was out in space somewhere.

Jeff lay down on his bed and pulled the covers up to his chin. At least he had a home. He looked at the drawing of the old man in the glow of his nightlight.

"He's probably homeless," Jeff thought. "Maybe he's sleeping in some cardboard box down by the creek. I hope not. Maybe tomorrow I'll go see him again."

Shivering, Jeff got up and walked out to where his mother was sitting.

"I forgot to tell you about what happened at school today," he began, then he noticed that her head was lying against the back of the sofa. She was sound asleep with the newspaper in her lap and the TV blaring away.

Jeff turned off the TV, wishing he could talk to his mother. His mom slowly opened her eyes.

"Oh, Jeff. What time is it?" She got up. "I'm so sleepy." She gave Jeff a quick hug. "Off to bed with you. Good night. See you in the morning."

He hoped he could sleep.

*It is one of the most beautiful
compensations of this life,
that no man can sincerely try to help
another without helping himself.
Ralph Waldo Emerson*

CHAPTER 9

The rest of the week at school was devoted to more tests. Jeff took his key and let himself into an empty house every afternoon. His best friend, Terry, sometimes walked part of the way with him, but most days he had swim practice and they couldn't play. Jeff drew every chance he got, and the memory of the blue jay that had taken over the class was his favorite thought.

By Friday afternoon, Jeff had made plans for his weekend. His mom always did her shopping on Saturday morning, and Jeff hated to go along. Instead, he'd decided to wait on the bridge for old Mr. Plaidcoat. He wanted to tell him about the blue jay. He was sure that it would make the sad, old man laugh too.

When he reached the path that led to the bridge, he thought he spied a figure walking toward him. Sure enough, it was the old fellow shuffling along. He hadn't seen him all week, and Jeff had wondered whether he would ever see him again.

As they slowly approached one another, Jeff noticed that the old man was carrying a fishing pole.

"Hi, Jeff. I thought I'd try my luck today from this bridge. You got a pole?"

"Yes," answered Jeff. "I've never fished from the bridge before, but I've thought about it lots of times."

The old man stuck something on the end of his hook and tossed the line into the water. They watched it land upstream and drift toward the bridge. Neither of them spoke. They were both concentrating on catching a fish. Finally, Jeff broke the silence.

"I wish you could have been at my school the other day."

"Oh, yeah. What happened?"

"This crazy blue jay flew in the window and took over the classroom."

"You mean that a bird actually flew right into your room?"

"Yep. Miss Radner was a basket case. She didn't know what to do with a wild bird loose. She was scrambling around the room trying to scare that bird back out the window, but it was impossible."

"That must have been something to see, all right."

"And not only that," exclaimed Jeff, "but it even managed to go to the bathroom on the achievement tests sitting on Miss Radner's desk."

The old man leaned his head back and laughed. "I guess that's what schools need these days. A few more wild birds bringing in a little of Mother Nature. What are those tests anyway? Don't believe we had those in my day."

"Lucky you. They stink. I hate them. We've been doing them all week. Boy, am I glad we have Saturday off."

His new friend was paying attention, and Jeff had lots to say. It seemed like nobody listened to him these days—not Miss Radner, not his mom, and not even Terry.

With a father in Alaska and a deserted house every day after school, Jeff was grateful to talk to this stranger standing by the water. This guy was like Grandpa. He could tell Grandpa anything.

"They always find out I'm stupid. They give me an answer sheet with little round circles, and I've got to answer page after page of questions so they can find out how much I know. I have trouble. Then my mom goes in, and they tell her I'm stupid. The teacher knows I'm stupid, and all the kids know I'm stupid. I don't know why they have to give those tests to me every year. I'm always just as stupid." A boy and his mother walked across the bridge.

"Wait a minute. You're not stupid. Don't you let them make you feel that way! Nobody with bright, shining eyes like yours could be stupid, and don't you forget it. You hear me? Don't you ever forget it!"

Jeff smiled. For a brief moment, he felt good. The old man handed him the fishing pole and said, "Reel it in, and you cast it out this time." A man stopped to watch them and then left.

Jeff quickly turned the handle and listened to the clicking sound of the retracting line. He checked the bait and moved his arm back to let the string go. It caught, and he said, "Oops." Then he tried again and was successful. The old man nodded his approval.

"Good one," he said.

Jeff felt proud. A baby cried as a mother pushed the stroller past Jeff and the old man, oblivious to any noise around them.

"I wish Dad could have seen that. Then he'd want to take me on his boat."

Jeff held on to the pole tightly as he looked over at his fishing buddy. He didn't know his real name. "Maybe he doesn't have a home," he thought, "but surely he has a name."

"What's your name?" he asked, curious to know more about the old man.

"Gramps. Just you call me Gramps."

"A perfect name," thought Jeff.

"Gramps," said Jeff, "last week I drew your picture."

The old man's eyes widened in a look of surprise. "You drew my picture. How about that. You drew my picture, eh? Now I'd call that an honor. Nobody ever drew my picture before—an old goat like me."

"You're not an old goat. Just old." They both grinned.

"Yep, I'm old, but I can still walk to the bridge and fish with my friend. Doesn't look like we're going to catch much today." They didn't give up though.

They took turns holding the pole, passing it back and forth every fifteen minutes or so. They were silent, listening only to the ripple of the water and the gentle rustle of the leaves blowing in the breeze.

Jeff recalled how excited he had been the first time he caught a fish. The best part was feeling the weight of it on his line. When he actually landed it on the dock, he was horrified to see it gasping and flapping. Somehow he'd never anticipated having to actually kill the fish.

He knew he was supposed to hit it over the head so it wouldn't suffer. He carefully dislodged the hook, trying not to tear the mouth and get blood on his shirt. Jeff gently released the struggling fish and watched it fight its way upstream after it hit the water.

His dad had teased him about it, so the next time he caught one he shut his eyes tightly and whacked it on the head with the bat. He didn't want to be a chicken. He couldn't eat it though. Just the thought made him gag. His mother had insisted that he clean the fish too. That was no picnic either. He pretended that he was Dr. Benson and that he had to operate. That was when he realized he never wanted to be a doctor. Too much blood and guts. The fish's eye stared at him the whole time.

Now he sat on his favorite bridge, fishing again with Gramps. He thought about his dad, catching tons of fish far away in Alaska. His dad didn't have to look at them one at a time. "That kind of fishing is different than this kind of fishing," he thought.

He hoped he wouldn't catch anything. He pictured some fish swimming by his line saying, "Sorry guys, I'm too smart for you."

"They outfoxed us today," said Gramps, taking Jeff's pole.

"There's always another day."

"Thanks for letting me use your pole."

Jeff knew his mother would be upset if she got home and found him gone.

"Good-bye, Gramps," he said, racing off toward home.

The old man slowly picked up all his gear and started down the path that led under the bridge.

Shall I tell you what knowledge is?
It is to know both what one knows
and what one does not know.
Confucius

CHAPTER 10

For the next few weeks, Jeff met Gramps at the bridge every day. Sometimes they'd fish, and sometimes they'd just talk.

Jeff learned that the old man lived alone in a houseboat about a mile from the bridge, near where the creek and the river met. He had a bad heart and had been told by his doctor to walk every day. That was why he came to the bridge so often. The old man didn't like walking much, but becoming friends with Jeff made the exercise easier.

Jeff told the old fellow how things were going at school. Nothing ever seemed as bad when he was telling Gramps as it did when it was happening.

Jeff didn't have to see the results of the test to know his scores would be low. They were always low.

There was no way around it. Jeff knew that he would have to confess to his mother again about how badly he'd done. He could already see her disappointed face.

"Some things are so dumb about tests, Gramps." Memories rushed into Jeff's head like water from a broken levee. He needed to talk.

"When I was in first grade, I cried at school. It was so embarrassing, and I never forgot it."

"What happened, Jeff? You can tell me."

"Well, during a test, the teacher said to put my marker under the first row. I thought I was doing what she said to do."

"I picked up the test and was trying to lay my marker underneath the first row. It was hard to tell where to put it. Some kids laughed when they saw what I was doing. She grabbed my marker and set it on top of the first row. After that I couldn't think. All I could hear were the kids laughing at me. She didn't say to put it on top. She said to put it under." Gramps put his hand on Jeff's head.

"Go on, tell me the rest."

"Another time, I was looking at these pictures on a test, and the teacher said to circle the things that were empty. There was a picture of a boy. She was upset when I asked her, 'Is that boy empty? I thought that maybe he didn't eat his breakfast.'

"She just said, 'Think again, Jeff,' as if I wasn't thinking at all. I was thinking, wasn't I, Gramps? I just wasn't thinking the way she was thinking."

"No question about it, Jeff. You were listening, and you were thinking both times." Sometimes tests prove very little, and leave people behind even when they're thinking.

We live and grow
by new knowledge.
Thomas Edison

CHAPTER 11

It was no fun being different. Teachers like the smart kids even when they're like Matt Huggins. He demanded all the attention. For instance, Miss Radner put up the pictures of Washington and Lincoln on Presidents' Day.

She asked, "Does anyone know who these people are?"

Matt yelled out, "I do, I do."

She usually didn't like it when anyone spoke so loud, but this time she just said, "Tell us, Matt. Who are they?"

"One's on the one dollar bill, and one's on the five dollar bill."

"She thought he was so clever," Jeff explained to Gramps. "I could have told her that much.

"I get scared when I have to take a test. My stomach hurts, and my eyes hurt, and sometimes, when I'm trying to figure something out, I think my head is going to blow up. I get all shaky on the inside and sometimes even on the outside.

"I've never told anyone before because I didn't want anyone to think I was different. I wanted to be like everyone else."

"You know, Jeff," said Gramps, "It sounds to me like you've got a bad case of test-o-phobia. That means you're beat before you even start. Fear can really get the best of you. You need a plan, a way to take charge. Right now those tests have got you buffaloed."

Jeff listened attentively. He needed some help, and it sounded to him like Gramps might have some.

"Everybody's afraid sometimes. You're not alone, Jeff. You just think you're alone. It's what you do with your fear that counts." Jeff listened with real attention.

"When I was a boy, there was one thing I was terrified of," Gramps continued, "and that was old Mr. Dever. He was my teacher in the fourth grade, and he was a mean son-of-a-gun. He didn't like me, and I didn't like him neither." Jeff thought that it was impossible that the old man had ever been in fourth grade.

"Every time something went wrong, old Dever blamed me. It got so even *I* believed I'd done half the stuff he accused me of doing. Why, he had his paddle, and he sure liked to use it."

"No paddles at my school," Jeff thought. "Poor Gramps. At least he lived to tell it."

"Why, I remember my very first day of school. I was all dressed up in my fancy knickers and cap when this big kid came up to me and grabbed my cap and threw it in the dirt. I picked it up and put it back on my head, and then he grabbed it again and threw it. Seeing that he was three times my size, I stooped down and retrieved the cap, brushed it off, and returned it to my head. He was persistent and came at me for a third time. But this time I'd had enough, so I threw myself on the ground and bellowed at the top of my lungs, 'Heeeelp,' until the principal came running out to see this poor little first grader crying at the feet of this huge bully.

"I'm happy to tell you that bully got what he had coming. It was all a matter of knowing when to ask for help."

Jeff listened attentively to Gramps as he told his story. "Wow! Life for Gramps was really tough," Jeff remarked to himself. Jeff started to think that maybe his problems weren't so bad after all. He knew he could handle Matt. They never actually fought with fists or anything.

"Sometimes, Jeff, you've got to fight fire with fire. Being afraid can get the best of you, if you let it, but you can always beat fear if you stare it in the face."

"I know, Gramps, that's true, and I'll try to remember that when I'm telling my mother that I failed again. Miss Radner hasn't said so, but I just know I did. That's the way it always is."

I say "try"; if we never try,
we shall never succeed.
Abraham Lincoln

CHAPTER 12

"I flunked again," said Jeff. "I'm sick and tired of the whole business. There's no point in asking Miss Radner how I did." Jeff stormed through the house and into his bedroom.

"Oh no," sighed his mother, keeping her voice low and trying not to react to his obvious disappointment. She decided to take him a sandwich and a glass of milk. She knew he wouldn't want to discuss the test results now.

She was absolutely right about that. Jeff ate, and then lay on his bed, looking up at the ceiling until he fell asleep. His sleep was not peaceful, because he had some weird dreams.

In his dream he was covered with feathers, standing on a bridge near a pile of stones. He was facing an enormous building, and he could see through its walls. Inside sat twenty kids, and they all looked exactly like Matt Huggins.

Jeff tossed and turned in his bed. He heard his mother yell "Stupid," as a rock sailed past him, shattering a glass and spewing pieces everywhere. He ran and hid himself in a cornfield among huge stalks of corn. There were crows flying and landing at his feet. He tried to catch them, but they were too quick.

Before he woke up, Jeff saw his father and his grandpa together. They both reached out to him for a hug, and he didn't want to wake up.

He woke, but he couldn't forget the dream. It was so vivid. In it, his grandpa had told him some things about his own frustration when he was in school. He had said, "I had to punch the chalkboard because of something they didn't like that they thought I did. I tried to knock Washington's picture off the wall by hitting as hard as I could. The picture swung, but it didn't fall."

Jeff could see this picture in his dreams and opened his eyes just as it was about to fall. He lay back down, trying to recall the dream. He wanted to talk to his mom. Quietly, he walked down the hall to her room, but she was sound asleep. He listened for a moment to her breathing and then crept back to his own bed.

"Face your fears," Gramps had said. "Stare them in the face." He hadn't tried to hide his failure from his mom, but he hadn't talked to her about it either. She had brought him a sandwich.

He waited until after school the next day to bring up the test subject to Miss Radner.

"I'd…I'd like to take that test again, please," stammered Jeff.

"This time I will read every question. Will that be okay?" It was almost more than Jeff could bear just to get the words out.

"Gramps said I should face my fears. He said that I shouldn't let tests get the best of me."

"You'd what?" asked Miss Radner, pushing her hair back from her ear as if to improve her hearing.

"I'd like to take that test again. I didn't read any of it, and I'd like to try to see if I can do better. I think I could do better if I wasn't so scared."

"Scared. You've been taking these tests for so many years now. Since kindergarten. Isn't it getting any easier?"

"No, no, no, Miss Radner. It's not easier for me. It's tougher and tougher and tougher. Every year, I get more scared. I get so nervous that I can't think. Then I try to just finish as fast as I can so that I can get it done before the other kids finish."

"How will I ever arrange for you to do that, Jeff? It's against standard procedure and administrative rules. It's not all up to me you know. When were you talking to Gramps?"

"Yesterday and all last week."

"I thought you told me your grandfather died last year. Isn't that so? So where did you get all this advice?" Her voice made Jeff hesitant to answer.

"Gramps," he said. "He's someone I met after school by the bridge." Jeff wasn't sure whether he should continue. After all, Gramps was a stranger, and that was the dreadful word that could cause him big trouble.

Jeff's head was ringing from her silence. By the way Miss Radner moved about the room, Jeff knew he wasn't going to get an answer out of her. He suspected that she was probably going to call his mother.

It was her manner that troubled Jeff, and the way she hastily turned and left the room, hurrying down the hall toward the principal's office.

True character
always pierces through
in moments of crisis.
Napoleon

CHAPTER 13

Sure enough, at seven thirty the phone rang, and Ruth Taylor responded by slowly dragging herself off the couch and heading to the kitchen where she took the phone off the hook and brought it to her ear.

"Hello," she said, without much enthusiasm. "Oh yes, Miss Radner." She immediately stood straighter and tried to sound calm. "I'm just fine. Thank you."

Jeff pulled himself up from where he lay drawing in front of the TV.

"I knew she'd call," Jeff thought. "I hope this isn't going to be the end of me. When Gramps said face it head on, he wasn't kidding. Here I go again."

He strolled through the doorway and stood near the kitchen sink. His mother began fidgeting with the telephone cord. Jeff noticed her expression change from calm to anxious. He knew his mother's worried look.

"Yes, he told me about the low score. Oh, I see. No, he didn't say anything about that to me." She moved from one foot to the other. Miss Radner was talking nonstop. Jeff's mom stared at him.

"No, I don't know anybody named Gramps. Jeff has said nothing to me about him. I'm very glad you called."

Jeff turned and ran quickly from the house. He needed to be alone. His mother would surely punish him for not going straight home after school. He needed to think. He wanted to convince her that what he had done was okay. But how?

He looked in the window and saw that his mother was still on the phone. He headed toward the path that led to the old Wilson house.

As Ruth Taylor hung the receiver back on the hook, she glanced around the room. "Jeff," she called. When there was no answer, she scrambled to get her shoes on and reached for her jacket. She nervously walked into his room, hoping he was there. She saw that he was not and sat on his bed to catch her breath.

"*Face your fears!*" Gramps's words rang in Jeff's ears. He turned around and headed back to the house. He could picture the sad look on his mother's face. He didn't want her to be sad. He thought about how she looked when his dad had left, and he didn't want to be responsible for giving her any more pain. He ran up the porch steps and opened the front door.

His mother was coming out of his room, looking confused and tired.

"We need to have a talk, Jeff. I guess you know I just had a call from your teacher."

"Who is Gramps?" Jeff could detect the tone of irritation in his mother's voice. He thought about his drawing of the old man.

"Well, he kind of looks like this. Wait just a minute." He bounded into his room and seized his drawing from the bed-side table, hurrying back to show his mom.

"Who is that in that drawing?"

"I met him down by the bridge," volunteered Jeff.

Jeff's mom put her hands to her temples in dismay. "And what have I told you about talking to strangers?" she asked.

"Oh, I know I shouldn't talk to strangers, but this is different."

"Different? No, Jeff, this is not at all different!"

Jeff hardly heard what she said as he continued, "You just have to meet him, Mom. He's terrific! I can't tell you about him, but you just have to meet him for yourself."

"Perhaps Miss Radner was right to be so concerned. This old man certainly has made an impression on you. And what's all this about taking a test over again? Did I hear that right?"

"I need another chance," Jeff replied. "Maybe I can do better. I want to try. Gramps thinks I can do better."

Jeff's mom had a flash of insight. Her own panic kept her from responding to Jeff's needs half the time. She was just so busy. Some fellow passing by on the bridge had taken time to listen and pay attention to Jeff in a way that she had not. She reached for Jeff's hand, and he didn't pull away.

"I'm so tired, Jeff. I like your drawing, and I'm sure you can do better on the test if given another chance. Just don't get your hopes up too much. It may not be possible."

To solve a problem
it is necessary to think.
It is necessary to think
even to decide
what facts to collect.
Robert M. Hutchins

CHAPTER 14

Early the next morning, Miss Radner confronted Principal Morrison with Jeff's request.

"I have a student, Jeffery Taylor, who would like to take his achievement test over again. What do you think?" she asked. Loaded down with papers she was carrying back to her room, she stood riveted, waiting for his answer.

Principal Morrison hesitated, scratched his head, rubbed his chin, then asked, "Do you think that would be fair to the others?"

"I don't know," she answered, "but he is so determined about it. I've been having some difficulty with him. He just doesn't listen, and he's such a daydreamer. This is such an attitude change that I hate to ignore it." Principal Morrison pushed his chair away from his desk.

"It really isn't something that we want to get started here. He will be taking the test again in the spring, and if word got out that we did it for one, it might cause problems. They might think we were trying to raise our test scores. Oh, you know the can of worms that might open."

Miss Radner shifted the papers in her arms and stepped toward the door.

"These tests are getting expensive, you know. We've got to watch the budget," he said. Miss Radner left Principal Morrison's office without saying another word. It was all decided. There would be no second test.

After lunch, Jeff approached Miss Radner's desk. "So what's the answer, Miss Radner?"

"You're not going to be too happy, Jeff. Principal Morrison doesn't think it's a good idea."

"Okay," replied Jeff. Secretly, he was glad because he didn't want to do it anyway. He had asked for it mostly because Gramps had suggested it. Miss Radner was a little disappointed that Jeff accepted her answer so easily.

"With a class as large as ours, it wouldn't be right to let you do what the others do not do," she continued, to satisfy herself.

"Right," said Jeff, not questioning Miss Radner any further. He wasn't sure that taking that stupid old test again would get rid of his fear anyway. Gramps thought so, but what did Gramps know? He had never taken one of those tests.

That afternoon, Jeff had lots of time to himself. He wandered down by the old Wilson house and hung around, kicking rocks. Then he headed for the bridge, thinking he might see Gramps. He had a special spot, which he called his fort, down under the bridge. He liked hearing the sound of the cars driving overhead. He and Terry went there often. They'd sit on the edge of the water on the cement area. It was a great hideout.

Today he took out his pencil and paper and drew everything he saw. He was careful about detail. He wished Terry could see his drawing. Tomorrow he'd show it to him. Terry didn't draw much, but he always liked what Jeff drew.

This was the first time that Jeff had drawn the hideout. Usually he spent time observing the ants doing work. They hauled stuff way bigger than they were and carried heavy loads to special places in the ground.

By watching them, Jeff understood how hard ants worked. In his desk at home, he had stacks of drawings of them. The ants helped him understand that through determination, one could get things done, no matter how small. The more he observed, the more he drew. The more he drew, the more he observed. Although Jeff learned by drawing, Miss Radner thought his drawing was play.

He got to draw during art class at school, usually on Fridays. But that wasn't enough for Jeff, so he stole moments here and there to doodle.

After rearranging some rocks to sit on and throwing a few of them in the water, Jeff decided that it was time to head for home. He recalled Miss Radner's stern face when she had given him an answer.

"I wonder what Gramps will say when I tell him Miss Radner said no." He wished Gramps had been at the bridge so they could have discussed it. His mother would want to know all about it too. He took the drawing of the hideout out of his pocket and examined it carefully. What a cool place to go.

Before he got to his front door, an idea struck him like lightning.

"That's what I'll do," he said aloud. "It's perfect." He decided to get his mother and Gramps both to come to his fort, and that's how they would meet. He couldn't keep a friend like

Gramps all to himself, and he couldn't give up a friend like Gramps. No way.

"I'm not allowed to take the test again," Jeff blurted out to his mother as soon as he saw her.

"I knew it," she sighed. "Rules are rules." Jeff was glad she didn't ask for details about what Miss Radner had said. He wanted to forget the whole subject.

"Mom," asked Jeff, "would you come to the bridge and see my fort? I know you have other things to do, but pleeease. It's such a cool place. It's not far from the Wilson house. Pleeease!"

It wasn't often that Jeff ever asked for anything, and his mom wanted to see where he was playing. "I hope you don't go on the porch at the old house. I heard they're planning to tear it down soon," she said.

"Will you come with me, Mom?" he asked, ignoring her comment about the porch.

"Sure, I'll try to get there by four o'clock, Jeff. I should be able to get off early." She felt confident that she could.

With any luck at all, Gramps would be at the bridge the next day, and Jeff could put his plan into action. He'd help Gramps down under to the fort and then go up and meet his mother and bring her down to meet him.

As Jeff crawled into bed that night, he thought about how their meeting would go. He knew his mother would like Gramps once she met him, and then Gramps wouldn't be a stranger anymore.

"What if he isn't at the bridge?" Jeff thought worriedly. "The whole plan will be ruined. Of course, he'll be there. He just has to be." Jeff buried his head in his pillow and tried to sleep.

If I have ever made any valuable discoveries,
it has been owing more to patient attention
than to any other talent.
Isaac Newton

CHAPTER 15

When the dismissal bell rang the following day, Jeff was the first one to scoot out the door. Coat flying, he pushed his way through the gate and headed for the bridge. Gramps was nowhere in sight. Disappointed, Jeff started for home, then spied the stocky figure walking slowly toward him. Delighted, he ran to him, grabbed his arm, and began talking and pulling at him at the same time.

"Let's go to the bridge, Gramps. You've got to see my hide-out. I'll take you there right now."

Trying to calm him a little, Gramps said, "Wait a minute, Jeff. What's your hurry? It isn't going to run away, is it?"

Only half-hearing Gramps's words, Jeff continued, "It's where Terry and I used to go, and I want you to see it. My mom is getting off work early today so she can see it too. I've got to run home and get her. Then you can meet each other."

It made perfect sense to him for his friend and his mom to meet in his fort. Gramps showed no resistance and smiled as Jeff guided him down the path that led to his special spot. It wasn't an easy walk, because there were roots and rugged areas and the old man wasn't that steady on his feet. But together they managed. Jeff was determined, and Gramps cooperated all the way.

"Say, this is quite a steep hiking place for a guy like me," Gramps chuckled.

Jeff stared a moment at his friend and wondered how he would ever climb down. "Here, give me your hand, Gramps. We'll make it, slow and easy."

There was a low spot, and Gramps had to maneuver carefully to keep from falling. "I see there are some rocks to sit on down here." With a few grunts and groans, Gramps succeeded in settling himself under the bridge.

"I'll just rest here while you go fetch your mother." Without saying a word, Jeff reached over and hugged Gramps. "What a guy," he thought.

Jeff ran up the side of the hill and scaled a low cement wall, taking a shortcut home to get his mom. He hoped that she would already be there, for he didn't want Gramps to have to sit for a long time on that hard rock. He had looked mighty uncomfortable.

Luckily, his mom was waiting in the hall ready to go when Jeff walked in the front door.

"Let's go, Mom. He's waiting in the hideout. I just know that you're going to like Gramps. He's so cool.

Gramps walks here almost every day. He has a bad heart, and it gives him exercise, walking this far from his house."

"What a lovely bridge this is, Jeff. I've always loved it. When your dad and I were first married, we came here on our evening walks. That was just before you were born. You probably like it so much because you remember the sound of the water. The rippling sound of the water was so relaxing, but sometimes you'd give me a little kick to let me know you were there."

Jeff had not heard that story before. He did like to hear the sound of the water, and he loved hearing about times when his mom and dad were together.

They continued on their way, moving toward a small path. In the distance was the abandoned old house.

"There's that forsaken place. I hate to think of you playing there alone."

"It's all right, Mom. I'm careful."

"No, Jeff. It just isn't safe. I should have checked on this. How could I be so stupid?"

"There he is, Mom. Right down there on that rock." Jeff was elated to see Gramps patiently waiting for them.

A silence followed as the boy and his mother gazed at the old man leaning against a piling. Jeff took his mother's hand to help her move closer.

"Mom, this is Gramps. Gramps, this is my mother," Jeff said, using all the manners he had been taught. The moment hung in the air waiting for Jeff's excitement to subside. Gramps's eyes met Mom's. Jeff looked from one to the other like he was watching a tennis match.

"Hello," said Ruth Taylor. "I'm happy to meet you. Jeff has told me so much about you that I'm glad for the chance for us to meet." She extended her hand. Gramps smiled and reached up to touch her hand as she bent down to sit.

"I'd offer you my rock," he said, "but I'm not sure I can get up." They both grinned.

"Never mind, Gramps. I'll just sit over here."

Jeff found comfort in seeing his mom and Gramps together. He knew she was right about strangers, but the truth was that Gramps was a pal. Sometimes you have to give some people a chance. If people treated everybody they didn't know as if they were nobody at all, life would be very lonely for some people. That's what Jeff often thought, and, after having met Gramps, he was sure of it.

Jeff moved away, for he needed a moment to himself. He scrambled up the bank to a green, grassy place. Billowy, white clouds moved overhead. Jeff hoisted himself up into the nearest tree. He had done his part to get those two together. The rest was up to them.

Let us have faith that right makes might,
and in that faith let us to the end
dare to do our duty as we understand it.
Abraham Lincoln

CHAPTER 16

Gramps hadn't been in a school building for years, but as a result of his conversation with Jeff's mom in the fort, he showed up at Jeff's school the next day. There was a determined look on his face as he headed for the principal's office.

All morning the old man thought about how destructive the present school system was to a kid like Jeff. It didn't leave room for creative thinking. It didn't allow for the Jeffs of this world to ever succeed. It didn't measure imagination, the stuff of invention and new ideas. It just measured book learning. It didn't leave room for sensitive teachers to cope. By the time he actually walked into the building, Gramps was steaming.

Ruth Taylor had arrived early. She and Gramps had made a deal while sitting under the bridge. Jeff was not going to face this alone year after year if they could help it. Together they would at least try to make a difference.

Jeff wanted to spend the day in his hideout, but he knew that was out of the question. He followed his mother down the hall as she walked toward Gramps.

They met near a large door labeled *Principal's Office*. They walked through the door, ready to speak to his secretary. Miss

Radner happened to be in the office picking up her daily attendance sheet.

"Good morning," she said, when she noticed them.

"Good morning," answered Ruth Taylor, standing straighter than usual and reflecting confidence unlike her.

"We would like to speak with the principal, please."

"Yes, of course," answered Miss Radner nervously.

"I believe that Principal Morrison is out checking on a maintenance problem, but he should be back shortly. Is there anything that I can do for you?"

"Yes, Miss Radner, I believe there is," said Gramps.

Ruth Taylor interrupted, "Jeff came home yesterday and informed me that he will not be allowed to take the achievement test again." Miss Radner took two steps toward the door.

Ruth Taylor continued, "We already know he has a real problem with testing, and we were hoping that he could learn to deal with the situation by having the opportunity to take it again." Ruth Taylor stepped forward. "It was very disappointing to hear that you had decided against it," she said.

Miss Radner hesitated for a moment, then smiled and said, "It was Principal Morrison's decision, mainly based on the idea that it is an unusual request and we could not possibly retest everyone." She thought to herself, "Where are you, Principal Morrison?" Since he was nowhere in sight, she continued, "You must understand that we are issued a limited number of tests and it does take away from other class learning. It's difficult to single out one child like this when we have so many."

Her polished delivery sent the blood rushing into Gramps's face. It was as though Old Dever had hit him with a board again.

"Why not single out one child," Gramps thought. "Every year they single him out by putting him in an embarrassing position that he has to deal with alone. One in which he hasn't a prayer of a chance of succeeding."

Gramps's mind was racing. "Now they won't even let him overcome his trauma because it gets in the way of their tidy little system." Gramps didn't want to say this to Miss Radner, for he could tell that she was just doing her job. But Principal Morrison was going to hear it all, because something needed to be said by someone. Jeff couldn't be the only child with this problem.

Ruth Taylor had to get to work, and Jeff left for class, but Gramps had all the time in the world. He located a chair in the corner and plunked down to wait for the principal's return.

As he walked into his office, Principal Morrison mumbled to himself about broken pipes in the boys' lavatory.

"Maintenance, never-ending maintenance problems," he muttered. He scarcely noticed the man sitting in the corner against the wall…sleeping.

It had been a long walk to the school for Gramps that morning, and it had tired him out. As he opened his eyes, he appeared disoriented and stood up. Principal Morrison stepped toward him and reached for his hand.

"Did you wish to speak to me about something?" he asked.

Gramps reached for his hand and tried to recall why he had come. Fortunately, the bell rang, and Gramps remembered.

Jeff's school. He had come to make them understand Jeff! The desire to defend Jeff returned, and Gramps ignored the uncomfortable feeling in the middle of his chest.

Jeff was his friend, and friends help friends. Gramps knew he had to convince Principal Morrison of the destructive thing that was taking place in his school. It was ruining Jeff's education.

An uncomfortable feeling progressed from a dull ache to a sharp pain under his breastbone. He caught his breath and gasped. Disregarding how he felt, he took a step closer to Principal Morrison and began to speak urgently.

"I'm not so educated as you, sir, but I'm smart enough to recognize a bad situation. Somebody has to speak out about what I'm gonna say."

Principal Morrison stared at Gramps's red face and saw the desperate look in his eyes. Listening was not his strong point because his position as principal required him to be the authority, but not today.

"Young years are important years. They never come back again. You ought to know that," said Gramps.

"Of course, I do," answered Principal Morrison, "But we're all about teaching here. That's what this school is about."

"Well your school's not doing much for Jeffery Taylor—just killing his spirit and making him feel dumb."

"I beg your pardon. We certainly do care about all of our students. We've been trying to teach Jeff some discipline," he added defensively.

"We have excellent teachers who have given hours of their time trying to get Jeff to do better. He just doesn't try hard enough. He doesn't pay attention. He's always daydreaming."

The room was quiet for a moment. Principal Morrison felt attacked, and he wasn't good at taking criticism.

"Who are you anyway?" Principal Morrison asked. "What do you really know about Jeff? Poor Miss Radner has struggled for months now. Without Jeff's cooperation, it's useless." Gramps wasn't buying it.

"Jeffrey Taylor is a fine boy," he began. "He sees some things real clear, and he understands more than you think. This whole test scheme has gone haywire. I just suppose a bunch of know-it-alls got together and decided that this was education. Just take control of what kids learn, how they learn, and how they should think. If they don't do well on a test, then too bad. They're stupid."

Principal Morrison moved behind his desk and sat down. He figured that Gramps wasn't finished, and he was right.

"It's a crime to care more about the tests than about the people taking them." Gramps rubbed his head. "I left school pretty early, myself, but I know all these tests can't be passed off as the most important thing in school. Some very bright kids are losing out here, and Jeff is one of them. He's scared of those tests." Gramps swayed a little to the left but didn't let that stop him. "Jeff doesn't think anybody cares about him. It's what he can produce that they care about. It makes me really mad to see one kid squelched by grown-ups who want to control everything for their own purposes."

By the time Gramps finished, he was sweating and short of breath. The room was spinning. He moved backward. He felt a crushing pang like an elephant sitting on his chest. It was the worst pain he had ever felt in his life. He stepped forward, grabbed his chest, and fell to the floor unconscious.

A life spent in making mistakes
is not only more honorable but
more useful than a life
spent doing nothing.
George Bernard Shaw

CHAPTER 17

The scream of the ambulance startled everyone, children and teachers alike. Everybody ran to the windows and doors to see what was happening.

"Line up for a fire drill," cried Miss Radner, and several other teachers scurried about determined not to let chaos rule.

Then they saw the medics carrying the stretcher from Principal Morrison's office. Jeff instinctively knew that something terrible had happened to Gramps. He knew he had to leave immediately.

"Miss Radner, I have to go home!" pleaded Jeff.

"No, you can't go without a note!"

Jeff did not listen. "I can't wait, Miss Radner. I have to leave now. Gramps needs me." He bolted out the door and didn't look back.

It was a small community, and Jeff knew where the hospital was located. It was a long walk, but he didn't care about that. He thought about Gramps's heart, and tears filled his eyes.

"He has to be all right," Jeff repeated to himself. "He just can't die."

Jeff was breathless when he arrived at the hospital. He saw the ambulance and looked around, trying to decide where to go. He wished his mother were with him, but that didn't stop him from entering the door that said "Emergency." He'd been there once before, when he'd broken his arm. He noticed several people in white moving in different directions. Busy people. There was a long empty hallway to one side and a high desk on the other. Florescent lights jumped at him. He hesitated, trying to decide which way to go. There was no sign of Gramps anywhere.

Stepping toward the high desk, he peered up at the lady who towered above him.

"I'm looking for Gramps. He's just been brought here in an ambulance. Can I see him?" he begged.

"Oh, is that old gentleman your grandfather?" she asked. "We need more information on him." Jeff stared, baffled by the size of the place and his own isolated feelings.

"An old gentleman arrived about twenty minutes ago, but we didn't have any identification on him except that he was visiting at the elementary school. No one seems to know him. He is your grandfather then?"

"No," said Jeff. "He's my friend. May I please see him?"

"He's in intensive care, and I can't allow anyone in there right now."

"Please," pleaded Jeff. "He needs me to be with him."

"One moment, please," she turned to answer her phone.

With that Jeff scurried down the hallway. Time was important. This nurse didn't realize that Gramps was expecting him to come, and Jeff wasn't going to let him down.

In such a small hospital, it was easy to find the Intensive Care Unit. Jeff located Gramps before anyone could stop him.

Overcome by the sight of so many strange contraptions, Jeff proceeded attentively into the room. His eyes quickly moved to the white bed sheets covering the motionless figure. Stepping closer, he touched the limp hand, then leaned his face very close to Gramps's ear.

"Hi, Gramps," he whispered. "It's me, Jeff. You're going to be just fine. I promise you that. We've got to go fishing again remember. We didn't catch that big one yet."

By noon, the school had informed Ruth that Jeff had left, and she hurried home and then to the hospital. Seeing her relieved Jeff, and as she hugged him he begged, "Let's stay with Gramps until we see that he's going to be okay. Please."

Ruth Taylor looked at Gramps and then at Jeff. How would she help Jeff if Gramps could not make it out of the hospital? She'd inquired about Gramps's condition, and it didn't look very hopeful.

"Jeff, Gramps may not go home," she said. "There isn't anything we can do for him. With rest, perhaps he will be fine. The body has a way of mending itself, but we can't stay here."

"Yes, we can, Mom. He'll get better if we stay. I just know he will, and I don't want to leave him. He might be scared when he wakes up in this strange place."

When Ruth Taylor looked at her son, she saw how important Gramps had become to him. She just couldn't ask Jeff to leave.

"You stay here. I'll see what I can do." Getting the doctors to agree to let Jeff stay was another story. They had hospital policy to deal with, and letting a nine-year-old boy stay with a dying old man might not be the best decision they had ever made. After having worked for an hour, beating on his chest and administering medications to him through machines, the doctors at Parkview Hospital started Gramps's heart beating, but he was still unconscious. If someone had begun CPR sooner, perhaps there would have been more hope. Time would tell. Reluctantly, they agreed to let Jeff and his mother remain in the Intensive Care Unit. For hours, they kept a silent vigil.

Jeff's mom slept off and on in the chair near the window, but Jeff, fighting his own tiredness, struggled to stay awake by drawing.

He pulled out several paper towels from the dispenser near the sink. He carefully smoothed them flat on the hospital service stand. Taking a pencil from his pocket, he began to draw a hospital bed. He put in all the metal parts, the cold, steel levers and other contraptions and gadgets that he had never seen before. He left nothing out except for the weak, dying figure on the bed.

Instead, he substituted a strong, vibrant Gramps sitting up in that bed and wearing a captain's hat. This Gramps was smiling at Jeff and telling him that this was the greatest day of his life.

Jeff had a vivid imagination. He felt exhilarated as he continued to draw the picture of an old man fulfilling his dream.

He had said he wanted to be the captain of a huge sailing vessel. Today he was ready to take that journey. Jeff turned the hospital bed into a giant ship with a huge sail perched on the wavy sea, and Gramps was standing aboard.

Although it didn't make much sense to him, Jeff knew his drawing was helping Gramps in some mysterious, unknown way.

Jeff didn't feel afraid or sad, for as he looked at the old man's face, he saw strength, courage, and a look of contentment. Continuously, he drew as if he and the paper were one. Every line was equally important.

Gramps died that night, but Jeff didn't lose him entirely, because Gramps had done something for him he would never forget. Gramps believed in him.

We must have eyes to see and ears to hear
and a mind that opens out to the life
and beauty of the world.
Nehru

CHAPTER 18

Life at school improved for Jeffrey Taylor after that. Seldom did his feelings of "being trapped" trouble him as they had before. It was as if he moved into another time-space, where he wasn't a victim anymore. Now he took charge of his work more, and even Matt Huggins noticed it and didn't bug him half as much. He remembered Gramps, and he toughened up and began to believe in himself.

"Perhaps we should spend more time preparing the children before they are tested," said Principal Morrison reflectively at the next teacher's meeting. Several workshops were dedicated to just that subject. Gramps's sudden heart attack at the school had affected all of them.

The next spring, Jeff had the opportunity to take the test again.

This time Miss Radner seemed less threatening to Jeff. As she handed out the test booklets, she said, "Take your time in getting started. Answer the questions you know first. There is no penalty for guessing. It will not count against you if you miss. You aren't expected to know everything. Just read it, and do your very best." She sounded more reassuring to Jeff.

"I can do some of this," he thought as the booklet was placed before him. He looked at the test, took a deep breath, and read the first sentence. He knew the answer. He proceeded. He knew many of the answers. There were some that he didn't know, and those he skipped, continuing on to the next question. He remembered what Miss Radner had said: "There is no penalty for guessing." When he finished a section, he went back and tried to solve the difficult questions. If he did not know the answers, he guessed.

He actually achieved more that day than ever before. He tried harder, and he knew Gramps's presence was close by. Halfway through the test, he understood that he wasn't doing it just for himself. He was doing it for Gramps too, and his mother would be so proud of him, but most of all he would be proud of himself. No more settling for half-trying.

Although Jeff still kept his clock by the bedside table, he seldom ever looked at it now, nor did he play with his miniature soldiers.

With his free time, he continued drawing. "You drew an old goat like me," Gramps had said. He loved that picture.

Jeff didn't get to do much art at school, but there was always home. His mother kept him supplied with tons of paper and pens. He drew from his imagination, and he drew objects he saw and people he knew. There was never any right or wrong in drawing, and that's why he liked it so much. His drawings were his own ideas on paper.

He started riding his bicycle every day and began doing tricks that scared his mother half to death. He was good at it and didn't fall.

A new chapter began for Jeff when his father returned from Alaska.

"I'll be staying here for a while," he said. He brought Jeff a blue and white sea captain's hat that he'd bought in a souvenir shop in Anchorage. Jeff loved that hat. He wore it everywhere. Now, at least, he got to see his dad sometimes.

"I'll be taking you out on the boat this summer if it's okay with your mother," he said. "Would you like that?"

Jeff stood ten inches taller as he tugged at his cap.

"Okay, Dad," he answered. "I really would. Can I go, Mom?"

Ruth Taylor calmly gave her permission. "Sure, Jeff. I won't stop you."

Frequently, Jeff wandered down to his fort under the bridge. It had new meaning for him now, and was still a favorite place to go. He remembered Gramps there, and, remembering Gramps, he never felt alone.

"I'm going out to sea, Gramps. My dad's taking me on his fishing boat." He sat down on the grass.

"Isn't that cool? I'm kind of scared though. It's a big ocean, and his boat is pretty small."

A gray and white seagull landed near the rock where Gramps had sat the day he met Jeff's mom. It looked at Jeff for a moment as if hesitant to leave.

"Are you here for Gramps?" Jeff asked, excited that he might be. The seagull lifted its head, hopped, then glided up into the blue sky, flying out toward the ocean.

Jeff recalled Gramps's words, "Face your fears." He pulled on his captain's hat and headed for home, ready to meet the open sea with his dad.

THE END

DISCUSSION QUESTIONS AND ACTIVITIES

Chapter 1

Thinking It Over

1.   What kind of person is Jeff?

2.   What doesn't he like about school?

3.   What do you know about Jeff's father? His mother?

4.   Why is the clock so important to Jeff?

5.   Does Jeff remind you of anyone you know?

Activities

Choose one of the following:

A. Art. Draw the main character of this story from the information given about him.

B. Writing. You are peeking into Jeff's clock. What do you see? What is happening?

Chapter 2

Thinking It Over

1. Why did Jeff want to sit in the front seat?
2. Why did his mother stop him?
3. How does Jeff cope?
4. Why does Jeff keep his key around his neck?
5. Why do you think he dreads school so much?

Activities

Choose one of the following:

A. Art. Sit in the backseat of your family car. Draw a picture of what you see.

B. Writing. Describe how you feel when you are sitting in the backseat of the car.

Chapter 3

Thinking It Over

1.   How does Miss Radner feel about testing?

2.   Why does Jeff's face turn red?

3.   Do you think Jeff is undisciplined?

4.   How does Miss Radner try to help Jeff?

5.   Why is drawing so important to Jeff?

Activities

Choose one of the following:

A. Art. Draw a picture of the part you like best in chapter 3.

B. Writing. Have you ever been teased like Matt Huggins teased Jeff? Write a paragraph about that.

Chapter 4

Thinking It Over

1.   Describe Jeff's feelings in this chapter.

2.   Why do you suppose Jeff does not like math?

3.   What is it that makes Jeff feel so trapped?

4.   How does Jeff escape?

5.   Does he complete the task Miss Radner gives him?

Activities

Choose one of the following:

A. Art. Find a nature book on spiders. Draw one with your own design.

B. Writing. Do a page of math. Write a paragraph telling how you felt while you were doing it.

Chapter 5

Thinking It Over

1. Does Jeff like to be alone?
2. Where does Jeff meet the old man?
3. Why does Jeff hesitate to talk to him?
4. Do you think Jeff should talk to him?
5. Why does Jeff put the clock to his ear?

Activities

Choose one of the following:

A. Art. Collect some small leaves. Fill a pan with water. Drop the leaves into the water. Watch how they land. Drop leaves onto a large sheet of paper. Glue them into a leaf collage.

B. Writing. Write a poem about a boy on a bridge.

Chapter 6

Thinking It Over

1. What was the first thing Jeff did when he got home?
2. Was drawing important to Jeff when he was alone?
3. Why did he draw the old man?
4. Does Jeff's mother understand Jeff?
5. Why did Jeff consider the clock and the old man's picture his friends?

Activities

Choose one of the following:

A. Art. Choose an object like a rock or a shell or a small favorite toy. Look at it carefully from all sides. Carry it in your pocket all day. Touch it. Think about it. That night draw a picture of it.

B. Writing. Write a short story in which your object helps comfort someone.

Chapter 7

Thinking It Over

1. What feelings do Jeff and Miss Radner share about testing?

2. How does Jeff cope with being a slow reader? Do you think that was a good idea?

3. Why does Jeff enjoy the bird so much?

4. How does Miss Radner handle the bird flying into the classroom?

5. Why do you think Jeff was so excited about the bird?

Activities

Choose one of the following:

A. Art. Find a bird feather if you can. Make a feather print. Experiment with ways to do this.

B. Writing. Make up a story about a boy or a girl and his or her pet bird.

Chapter 8

Thinking It Over

1. What did Jeff not want to watch on TV?
2. Where is Jeff's father?
3. How do you think Jeff feels with his father so far away?
4. Why is Jeff's mother so tired?
5. Do you think Jeff's father cares about Jeff?

Activities

Choose one of the following:

A. Art. Do a finger painting of the ocean.

B. Writing.

- Write a letter to Jeff as if you were his father.
- Write a letter to Jeff as if you were his mother.

Chapter 9

Thinking It Over

1. Why did Jeff not go swimming with his friend Terry?
2. Did Jeff like fishing? If so, why do you think he did?
3. Was the bridge in a deserted location? How do you know?
4. Did Gramps help Jeff? How?
5. Did Jeff help Gramps? How?

Activities

Choose one of the following:

A. Art. Draw a picture of Gramps and Jeff fishing from the bridge. Include fish under the water.

B. Writing. Ask your parents to tell you a story about their childhood. Write it down.

Chapter 10

Thinking It Over

1. Where did Gramps live?

2. What had Gramps wanted to be when he grew up?

3. Why did Gramps come to the bridge every day?

4. How did Jeff do on his test?

5. How did Gramps help Jeff deal with his low score?

Activities

Choose one of the following:

A. Art. Find a picture of a houseboat. Draw a scale model of the inside.

B. Writing. Think about something that you dream about doing in your future. Write it down in detail.

Chapter 11

Thinking It Over

1. Why do you think Jeff doesn't want to be different?

2. What is test-o-phobia?

3. Who was Mr. Dever?

4. How did the bully get caught in Gramps's story?

5. What do you think Gramps meant by "fighting fire with fire"?

Activities

Choose one of the following:

A. Art. Draw ten people that are alike. Now draw one that is different.

B. Writing. Write something that you like about yourself that is different.

Chapter 12

Thinking It Over

1. Did Jeff try to hide his failure on the test from his mother?

2. What was his dream?

3. Did Jeff want to solve his own problem? How do you know this?

4. What did Jeff say to Miss Radner when he went to see her?

5. What did Miss Radner do about what Jeff told her?

Activities

Choose one of the following:

A. Art. Draw an illustration of Jeff's dream.

B. Writing. Write about a dream that you have had.

Chapter 13

Thinking It Over

1. Why did Jeff run out of the house?

2. Why did he quickly return to the house?

3. Why was Jeff's mother so upset?

4. Why did Jeff want to take the test again?

5. Does Ruth Taylor learn something about herself in this chapter? If so, what is it?

Activities

Choose one of the following:

A. Art. Lay on the floor and draw a picture of anything.

B. Writing. Write twenty of the longest words in this chapter.

Chapter 14

Thinking It Over

1. Why did Principal Morrison decide not to let Jeff take the test?

2. Did Jeff care?

3. Where was Jeff's fort?

4. What was Jeff's idea?

5. Why do you think Jeff wants his mother to go to the fort?

Activities

Choose one of the following:

A. Art. Draw an ant colony busy at work or your favorite imaginary fort.

B. Writing. Find an insect out-of-doors. Watch and write a story about what you see.

Chapter 15

Thinking It Over

1. Why do you think Jeff wanted his mother and Gramps to meet in his fort?

2. Do you think taking Gramps to the fort was a good idea?

3. What did Jeff's mother think of the old Wilson house?

4. What did Jeff's mother say about the bridge?

5. Why do you think that Jeff left his mother and Gramps alone in the fort?

Activities

Choose one of the following:

A. Art. Make an interesting card for a friend.

B. Writing. Write a description of a place where you like to sit by yourself.

Chapter 16

Thinking It Over

1.   What was the decision Gramps and Jeff's mother made while under the bridge?

2.   Why do you think Jeff's mother was so confident at the school that day?

3.   Do you think Jeff's mother and Gramps should have stayed out of it?

4.   Does the principal believe that he is doing the best for the students?

5.   What does Gramps believe about this situation? What happens to him at the end of the chapter?

Activities

Choose one of the following:

A. Art. Do a finger painting that expresses anger.

B. Writing. Write a paragraph about anger you had and about how you handled it.

Chapter 17

Thinking It Over

1. How did Jeff get to the hospital?
2. How do you know that Jeff lives in a small community?
3. What was wrong with Gramps?
4. Why did Jeff want to stay with his friend?
5. How did drawing help Jeff?

Activities

Choose one of the following:

A. Art. Draw your version of Jeff's picture.

B. Writing. Describe an emergency in which you saw someone hurt.

Chapter 18

Thinking It Over

1. What does that mean to you that *Jeff was a survivor*?
2. What happened to Gramps?
3. Did Jeff take the test again? If so, how did he do?
4. What happened when Jeff's dad returned from Alaska?
5. What did Jeff learn from this story?

Activities

Choose one of the following:

A. Art. Draw a picture of Jeff in his father's boat.

B. Writing. What did you learn from this story?

TEST TAKER TIPS

What to do during the test:

1. Allow yourself "panic time." Time to notice how you feel.
2. A little tension is good—makes you more aware.
3. When handed the test, turn it over on your desk.
4. Breath deeply—relax.
5. Pay attention to the directions.
6. Find out whether there is a penalty for guessing.
7. Scan the whole test before you begin.
8. Begin where you want to begin with the easiest questions first.
9. If you are stuck, move on.
10. Praise yourself. Talk to yourself in a positive way. "I am doing a great job on this test. I have lots of tools that will help me remember the answers."
11. If you have time, check your work.

978-0-595-38293-4
0-595-38293-2

Printed in the United States
59087LVS00006BA/535-633